My Weirder School #12

Mrs. Lane Is a Pain!

Dan Gutman

Pictures by
Jim Paillot

HARPER
An Imprint of HarperCollinsPublishers

To Miriam Chester

My Weirder School #12: Mrs. Lane Is a Pain!

Text copyright © 2014 by Dan Gutman

Illustrations copyright © 2014 by Jim Paillot

Library of Congress Cataloging-in-Publication Data

Gutman, Dan.

Mrs. Lane is a pain! / Dan Gutman ; pictures by Jim Paillot. – First edition.

pages   cm. – (My weirder school ; #12)

ISBN 978-0-06-219848-8 (lib. bdg.) – ISBN 978-0-06-219847-1 (pbk. bdg.)

[1. Schools–Fiction.   2. Talent shows–Fiction.   3. Humorous stories.]   I. Paillot, Jim, illustrator.   II. Title.

PZ7.G9846Msg   2014   2013051282

[Fic]–dc23   CIP

                                                                      AC

Typography by Kate Engbring

14 15 16 17 18   CG/RRDH   10 9 8 7 6 5 4 3 2 1

❖

First Edition

Contents

The Coolest Sport Ever

My name is A.J. and I hate getting hit by water balloons.

Do you and your friends ever have water balloon jousts? Water balloon jousting is the coolest sport ever. Especially when you joust on bikes.

One time we were having a water balloon joust on the grassy field next to our school. My friend Alexia and I were the knights. We got on our bikes at opposite ends of the field. Our friends Ryan and Michael were the squires. Squires are people who help the knights. Neil, who we call the nude kid even though he wears clothes, was the judge. He put a line of orange cones on the grass so Alexia and I wouldn't crash into each other.

I put on my bike helmet. Alexia put on her helmet.

"Hand me my water balloon, squire," I told Michael.

"Yes, my liege."*

---

* I don't know what a liege is, but that's what squires are supposed to say whenever knights say anything to them.

Michael handed me a big red water balloon. Ryan handed Alexia a blue water balloon at the other end of the field.

"Are the knights ready?" shouted Neil.

"Ready!" I shouted.

"Ready!" Alexia shouted.

"On your mark . . . ," yelled Neil. "Get set! Joust!"

Kids, please don't try this at home. We're professionals.

Alexia and I started pedaling toward each other. It's not easy to pedal a bike on the grass while you're holding a water balloon in one hand.

We were getting closer to each other.

I held up my water balloon, ready to let it fly.

Alexia and I were twenty feet away from each other.

"Nail him, Alexia!" shouted Ryan.

"You can do it, A.J.!" shouted Michael.

Alexia and I were ten feet away from each other.

It's really hard to hit somebody with a water balloon from a moving bike. You have to throw it at the exact perfect moment.

Alexia and I were five feet away from each other. It was time.

"EEEEE-YAH!" I hollered.

Just as I was about to let go of my water balloon, Alexia heaved her balloon. It exploded all over me. I was *soaked*. My

water
balloon
sailed
wide,
missing
Alexia entirely.

"Bam!" Alexia
hollered as she
rode by. "In your
face, A.J.!"

"Alexia is the winner!" shouted Neil.

After that we switched places so Michael
and Ryan would be the knights and Alexia
and I would be their squires.

It was a blast! I got nailed three or four
times, but I hit Alexia a few times, too.

Everybody was drenched and falling-down laughing. We kept jousting until we ran out of water balloons.

That's when the most amazing thing in the history of the world happened. I noticed that somebody was hiding behind the bushes nearby.

Well, that's not the amazing part, because people hide behind bushes all the time. The amazing part was *who* was hiding behind the bushes.

I figured the person watching us was Andrea Young, this annoying girl in my class with curly brown hair. But it wasn't Andrea. You'll never believe in a million hundred years who was spying on us.

It was Mr. Klutz, our school principal!

He has no hair at all. I mean *none*. He must save a lot of money on shampoo and combs. I wonder if he uses a hair dryer to dry his head.

"Uh-oh!" I said. "It's Mr. Klutz!"

"We're in trouble now," said Ryan.

Mr. Klutz came over to us. It was too late to run away. I didn't know what to say. I didn't know what to do. I had to think fast.

"We're sorry, Mr. Klutz," I said. "We won't do it again."

"Please don't tell our parents we were jousting with water balloons," begged Neil the nude kid.

"Don't be silly!" said Mr. Klutz with a big smile on his face. "I really enjoyed watching you. In fact, you kids have given me a great idea."

"We have?" said Alexia.

"What's the great idea?" asked Michael.

"I'm not going to tell you," said Mr. Klutz.

"Please? Please? Please? Please?" we all begged.

Usually, if you say "please" over and over again, grown-ups will get sick of hearing it and give you what you want. That's the first rule of being a kid.

"Okay, okay, I'll tell you my great idea," said Mr. Klutz.

"Yay!"

"I'll tell you my great idea . . . at the assembly tomorrow."

"Boo!"

The Secret Grand Prize

The next morning our class had to walk a million hundred miles to the all-purpose room for the assembly. Andrea was the line leader. Her crybaby friend Emily was the door holder.

I don't know why they call it an assembly because we don't put anything together.

If you ask me, they should make assemblies and toys the same way: no assembly required.

I sat next to Ryan and Michael. Everybody was gabbing, like always. Even the teachers. When Mr. Klutz climbed up onstage, he made a peace sign with his fingers, which means "shut up."

"Good morning," Mr. Klutz said. "I was watching some of our students playing on the field after school yesterday, and it gave me a great idea."

"Maybe he's going to give us an award or something," I whispered to Ryan.

"That would be cool," he replied.

"I realized how talented you students are here at Ella Mentry School," said Mr. Klutz, "so I've decided that we're going to have a talent show! We're going to call it *Ella Mentry School's Got Talent*!"

WHAT?!

"Yay!" said all the girls.

"Boo!" said all the boys.

"Talent shows are for girls!" I shouted.

"Yeah," agreed all the boys.

"I'm not going to be in some dumb talent show," said Ryan.

"Me neither," said Michael.

"Oh, I should mention one thing," said Mr. Klutz. "The winner of the talent show will get a secret grand prize. So if none of the boys will be participating, I guess a girl will win the secret grand prize."

Secret grand prize? I *love* secret grand prizes!

"Where do I sign up?" I shouted.

"You can sign up right here in the all-purpose room after school today," said Mr. Klutz. "But right now I want to introduce the woman who is going to be in charge of our talent show. She's a real professional talent coach, and her name is . . . Mrs. Penny Lane!"

At that moment, the weirdest thing in

the history of the world happened. A lady came out on the stage.

Well, that's not the weird part, because ladies come out on the stage all the time. The weird part was that she came out on the stage riding a *unicycle*. Not only was she riding a unicycle, but at the same time she was juggling three goldfish bowls, with real live goldfish in them! And not only was she riding a unicycle and juggling three goldfish bowls, but she was also whistling "Old MacDonald Had a Farm."

"WOW!" everybody said, which is "MOM" upside down.

It was totally amazing! Mrs. Lane is *really* talented!

The Talented Mrs. Lane

Mr. Klutz told us to give Mrs. Lane a round of applause, so we all clapped our hands in circles.

"Howdy, y'all!" said Mrs. Lane as she took a deep bow.

She must be from Texas. People in Texas say "y'all" all the time. Nobody knows why.

"Mrs. Lane is the perfect person to run our talent show," Mr. Klutz told us. "As you can see, she's very talented herself. In fact, you may have seen her on TV."

Everybody got all excited, because anybody who's on TV must be really famous. Mr. Klutz asked Mrs. Lane to tell us some of the TV shows she'd been on.

"Well," she said, "I was a contestant on *America's Not Stupid, Are You Smarter Than a Turnip?, America's Next Top Garbage Collector, Keeping Up with the Librarians, Who Wants to Win a Million Pizzas, Pancake Wars, Wheel of Misfortune,* and *Undercover Mother.*"

"WOW," everybody said again.

"Mrs. Lane is a real celebrity!" said Andrea. "She's *famous*."

Mr. Klutz asked Mrs. Lane if she had any *other* talents. She got off the unicycle and did a handstand while singing "I've Been Working on the Railroad."

"WOW," everybody said again.

We gave her another round of applause. Mrs. Lane was all out of breath.

"That was *amazing*!" said Mr. Klutz. "You are *multi*talented, Mrs. Lane."

Multitalented means "many talents." I knew that because every morning my mom gives me a multivitamin. It has ten different vitamins in it. How do they jam all those vitamins into one pill? Nobody knows.

"I'm so excited to be in charge of *Ella Mentry School's Got Talent,*" said Mrs. Lane. "This is going to be so much fun! Your brothers and sisters will be there. Your parents will be there. You might even get in the newspaper."

"Does anybody have any questions for Mrs. Lane?" asked Mr. Klutz.

Ryan raised his hand.

"Do armpit

farts count as a talent?" he asked.

"What's an armpit fart?" asked Mrs. Lane.

All the boys started making armpit farts. With hundreds of us doing it at the same time, it sounded like an orchestra. Except with armpits instead of musical instruments.*

"Yes, I *suppose* that would qualify as a talent," said Mrs. Lane.

"How about regular farts?" I asked.

"No," said Mr. Klutz firmly. "Regular farts do *not* qualify as a talent."

"That's not fair!" somebody shouted.

"Yeah, if armpit farts are a talent, then *real* farts should be a talent, too," said Neil the nude kid.

"That's discrimination against certain kinds of farts!" said Alexia. "And we were taught that discrimination is wrong."

"Yeah!"

---

* That would be cool if there was an orchestra of armpit farters.

Everybody started talking about farting and discrimination until Mr. Klutz made the shut-up peace sign again.

"Are there any questions that don't concern farting?" he asked.

Emily raised her hand.

"What if somebody doesn't *have* a talent?" she asked. "Does that mean they can't be in the talent show?"

Mrs. Lane came down off the stage and went over to Emily.

"*Everybody* has talent, sweetie," she said. "I'm sure y'all can do something that most other people can't do. For instance, maybe y'all can play the spoons."

Mrs. Lane pulled two spoons out of her pocket and started hitting them against her legs in rhythm. It was cool.

"I can't do that," said Emily.

"Well, maybe y'all can yodel," said Mrs. Lane.

Mrs. Lane started yodeling. It was cool.

"I can't do that either," said Emily.

"Or maybe y'all can turn your eyelids inside out," Mrs. Lane said. And then she turned her eyelids inside out.

Ewww, gross! I thought I was gonna throw up.

"I can't do that either," said Emily.

"I bet y'all are talented at *something*," Mrs. Lane told Emily. "Y'all just have to find out what it is."*

With that she picked a hula hoop up

---

* Boy, she sure says "y'all" a lot.

from the stage and started hula hooping while reciting the Gettysburg Address in a Donald Duck voice.

Mrs. Lane is weird.

No Talking, Please

We walked a million hundred miles back to our classroom with our teacher, Mr. Granite. Neil was the line leader. Michael was the door holder.

"This is so exciting!" said Andrea. "I can't wait to be in *Ella Mentry School's Got Talent*."

"Maybe I'll do some magic tricks," said Michael. "I got a magic kit for Christmas."

"I'm going to do some tricks on my skateboard," said Alexia. "That's a talent."

"No talking, please," said Mr. Granite.

"I could play the violin," said Neil the nude kid.

"I could eat something that isn't food," said Ryan.

"Eating isn't a talent," said Andrea.

"That depends on what you eat," said Ryan.

"If armpit farts can be a talent," said Michael, "then eating can be a talent, too."

"No talking, please," said Mr. Granite.

"What are *you* going to do in the talent

show, A.J.?" Neil asked me.

I really didn't know. I couldn't sing or dance or do magic tricks. But that's when I came up with the greatest idea in the history of the world.

"I could tell jokes!" I said.

"Oh, yeah?" said Andrea. "Let's hear one."

"What's the difference between snot and broccoli?" I asked.

"What?" everybody said.

"Kids will eat snot."

"That's disgusting, Arlo, and it's not funny," said Andrea. "It's not even a joke. It's a riddle."

"No talking, please," said Mr. Granite.

What is Andrea's problem? If being annoying is a talent, she's the most talented kid in the world. Why can't a truckful of broccoli fall on her head?

"I don't know what I can do in the talent show," said Emily. "I don't have a talent."

I felt a little sorry for Emily. It's sad to have no talent at all. But she *is* annoying, so I didn't feel *that* sorry for her.

"I know what *I'm* going to do in the talent show," said Andrea. "I'm going to sing a

medley of songs from the musical *Annie*."

Oh no, not *again*!

Andrea loves that show *Annie*, and she never misses the chance to sing songs from it. She sings songs from *Annie* every day. If I have to listen to "Tomorrow" one more time, I think I'll go crazy.

"Can I sing with you in the talent show, Andrea?" asked Emily.

"I prefer to sing solo," Andrea replied.

"Why don't you sing so low that we

can't hear you?" I told Andrea.

"Oh, snap!" said Ryan.

"No talking, please," said Mr. Granite.

I don't get it. For the first few years of your life, all grown-ups do is teach you how to talk. And then, for the rest of your life, all they do is tell you to stop talking. What's up with that?

Next!

The last thing I want to do after school is to stay after school. But this day was different. As soon as the three-o'clock bell rang, the gang and me rushed to the all-purpose room to try out for *Ella Mentry School's Got Talent*.

I don't know why they call it the

all-purpose room. It can't be used for *all* purposes. I mean, you can't go skydiving in there.

Anyway, lots of kids in all the grades from first through fifth showed up to try out. We had to wait in line behind a bunch of first-grade Munchkins so we could write our names on the sign-up sheet.

"I see we have a lot of talented students at Ella Mentry School," said Mrs. Lane. "I can't wait to see y'all show your talent!"

Mr. Klutz was there too. I guess he wanted to make sure nobody tried to do an act that involved farting.

"Can you tell us what the secret grand

prize will be?" asked Andrea, who loves to win prizes.

"If I told you, it wouldn't be a secret," Mrs. Lane replied.

She took the sign-up sheet and sat in the front row. Each of us had one minute to do our act.

"Okay," Mrs. Lane said to the first kid on the list. "Show me what you've got."

It was a second-grade girl with red hair. She said she was double jointed. Then she got down on the floor and wrapped

both of her legs around her neck at the same time.

That's a talent? Who knew?

"Next!" shouted Mrs. Lane.

Two fourth-grade boys climbed up onstage and acted out a scene from *Star Wars*. It ended with them fighting with light sabers. That was pretty cool.

"Next!"

A girl from the first grade came out.

"I can name all the months of the year that have the letter *Z* in them," she said.

"None of the months of the year have a *Z* in them," Mrs. Lane told the girl.

"There! I did it!"

"Next!"

"I can write my name in the air with my butt," said this first-grade boy.

"Next!"

After that some fifth graders did a skit about four bananas that go out for a walk and are suddenly attacked by meteors. It made no sense at all. They were followed by a bunch of clumsy girl dancers, bad lip-synchers, terrible rappers, and a dumbhead who spun plates on a stick.

I slapped my head. Man, those acts were *horrible*! They should call the show *Ella Mentry School's Got No Talent*. It was going to be a cinch for me or one of our gang to win the secret grand prize. But we had to sit through all the dumb acts. It was taking a million hundred hours.

I had looked up a few jokes in a joke book I had in my backpack, but I didn't know if they were funny or not. I was getting nervous.

"Next!" shouted Mrs. Lane.

Michael got up onstage and did a magic trick where he made some flowers pop out of his sleeve. It was cool.

"Want to see me make a candy bar disappear?" asked Michael.

"Sure," said Mrs. Lane.

Michael took a candy bar out of his pocket and ate it.

"See?" he said. "I made it disappear!"

"Next!"

Ryan came out.

"I can communicate with dolphins," he said.

"Do you have a dolphin with you?" asked Mrs. Lane.

"No," Ryan said. "I talk with them on the phone."

"Next!"

It was Emily's turn. She looked even more nervous than me.

"I would like to do a dance from *The Little Mermaid*," she said.

Emily started to dance, and to tell you the truth, she wasn't all that bad. But right in the middle, she spun around and fell down.

It's funny when people fall down. Nobody knows why. I tried not to laugh, because it's not nice to laugh when people fall down. And when they start crying, like Emily did, it's not funny at all.

Mrs. Lane came up onstage and put her arm around Emily.

"You know, I fell down just like that

when I was on *America's Not Stupid,*" she
said.

"You did?" Emily said, wiping her eyes.
"What happened?"

"Everybody laughed at me," said Mrs.
Lane. "I was humiliated. And I messed up
when I was on *Are You Smarter Than a*

Turnip?, too. It's okay to mess up. We all do it."

Emily stopped crying. Mrs. Lane went back to her seat in the front row.

"Next!" she shouted.

Some kid came out and burped the whole alphabet in ABC order. It was gross, but also hilarious.

"Next!"

Andrea sang the "Tomorrow" song. It was totally lame.

"Next!"

Finally it was my turn. I was nervous when I climbed up on the stage.

"I would like to tell some jokes," I said.

"Go ahead, A.J.," said Mrs. Lane.

"Why did the monkey fall out of the tree?" I asked.

"Why?" everybody replied.

"Because it was dead!" I said.

Nobody laughed. I guess this crowd doesn't go for dead-monkey jokes. I tried another one.

"I like to study for tests underwater," I said. "Maybe that's why I'm below C-level."

Nobody laughed.

"Get it?" I asked. "C-level? Sea level?"

Maybe I should have tested my jokes out in advance. My forehead was starting to sweat.

"Thirty seconds, A.J.," said Mrs. Lane.

"Did you know that I have holes in

my underwear?" I asked. "Well, how else would I get my legs into them?"

Nobody laughed. I thought I heard the sound of crickets out in the all-purpose room.

This was terrible! Usually, all I have to do is say the word "underwear" and kids start laughing.

"Next!"

When everybody was finished, Mrs. Lane stood up and gave us a standing ovation.*

"I really loved your acts," she said. "Y'all should rehearse as much as possible

---

* Well, I guess she couldn't have given us a standing ovation if she was still sitting down.

43

before the talent show next week. Oh, before you go, I have some news for y'all. There's going to be a surprise guest at the talent show."

"Did you hear that?" Andrea shouted. "There's going to be a surprise guest at the talent show!"

"There's going to be a surprise guest at the talent show!"

"There's going to be a surprise guest at the talent show!"

In case you were wondering, everybody was saying there was going to be a surprise guest at the talent show.

"Who will the surprise guest be?" asked Alexia.

"If I told you, it wouldn't be a surprise," said Mrs. Lane.

I love surprises, because you never know what's going to happen. That's why they're called surprises.

I was sure that the surprise guest was going to be Mr. Hynde. He used to be our music teacher, but then he made a hit rap record and became famous.

"Okay, let's call it a day," said Mrs. Lane. "Y'all work on your acts, and I'll see y'all at rehearsal tomorrow. Be here at four o'clock sharp."

Fantastic News!

I showed up the next day for rehearsal at four o'clock sharp. The only problem was that Mrs. Lane wasn't there.

"Where's Mrs. Lane?"

"Where's Mrs. Lane?"

"Where's Mrs. Lane?"

In case you were wondering, everybody

was asking where Mrs. Lane was.

We waited around for a million hundred minutes. Something was definitely wrong.

"I hope Mrs. Lane is okay," said Emily, who worries about everything.

You'll never believe who walked into the door at that moment.

Nobody! It would hurt if you walked into a door. But you'll never believe who walked into the door*way*.

It was Mr. Klutz!

"Where's Mrs. Lane?" we all asked him.

"She's not coming in today," he told us. "I had to fire her."

WHAT?

"I'm sorry to tell you this," Mr. Klutz

said, "but *Ella Mentry School's Got Talent* is canceled."

"*WHAT?*" everybody shouted.

"I had no idea how much money it costs to put on a show like that," said Mr. Klutz. "We need to hire a professional lighting-and-sound company. We have to pay for extra security. We have to get a permit from city hall to keep the school open at night. We have to print up programs. And of course we have to pay Mrs. Lane. It's all very expensive. We just don't have that much money in the school budget."

Bummer in the summer!

"I was just starting to get excited about the talent show," Ryan said.

"Me too," said Michael.

Everybody was sad. We started gathering up our stuff to go home.

"I'm sorry, kids," Mr. Klutz said. "Maybe we'll have a talent show next year."

But you'll never believe who walked into the door at that moment.

Nobody! I thought we went over that already.

Mrs. Lane came walking in the doorway. She was balancing a baseball bat on one foot at the same time as she was balancing an egg on a spoon in her mouth. It was amazing!

"I have fantastic news, y'all!" she shouted. "A company is going to sponsor *Ella Mentry School's Got Talent*!"

"Yippee!" everybody shouted.

"Sponsor?" I asked. "What does *that* mean?"

"It means they're going to give us the

money we need to put on the show," said
Mrs. Lane.

"Yippee!" I shouted. "What company?"

"Porky's Pork Sausages," she told us. "I
just got off the phone with the owner of

the company, Mr. Porky."

"Well, if that's true," said Mr. Klutz, *"Ella Mentry School's Got Talent* will go on as scheduled."

"Yippee!" everybody shouted.

"Hooray for Porky's Pork Sausages!"

"They saved the talent show!"

"Okay," said Mrs. Lane. "I'll see y'all at four o'clock sharp tomorrow for rehearsal."

Who Needs TV?

I showed up for rehearsal at four o'clock sharp the next day. And guess what? Mrs. Lane wasn't there. Again!

"Where's Mrs. Lane?" asked Alexia.

"Where's Mrs. Lane?" asked Neil the nude kid.

"Where's Mrs. Lane?" asked Michael.

In case you were wondering, everybody was asking where Mrs. Lane was. But then she came in. She was jumping on a pogo stick while dribbling a basketball and playing "Mary Had a Little Lamb" on a harmonica, all at the same time. It was amazing!

"I have fantastic news!" she shouted. "Are you ready for this? Mr. Porky of Porky's Pork Sausages just told me he's going to put *Ella Mentry School's Got Talent* on TV!"

The girls started screaming.

"EEEEEK! We're gonna be on TV!"

"We're gonna be on TV!"

"We're gonna be on TV!"

In case you were wondering, all the girls were saying we were gonna be on TV.

Being on TV must be the greatest thing in the history of the world. I've seen people jump into pools full of mud to get on TV. I've seen people eat bugs to get on TV. People will do *anything* to get on TV.

Mr. Klutz came running in with three of the teachers: Ms. Hannah, Mrs. Roopy, and Miss Small.

"We heard *Ella Mentry School's Got Talent* is going to be on TV," shouted Ms. Hannah, our art teacher. "Can we be in it too? I can make finger shadows of circus animals."

"I can play the nose flute," said Miss Small, our gym teacher.

"I can do impersonations of nursery rhyme characters," said Mrs. Roopy, our librarian.

"Yes, teachers can participate," said Mrs. Lane. "But there's something I need to talk to y'all about. Mr. Porky has three demands that must be met before he agrees to put *Ella Mentry School's Got Talent* on TV."

"What are his demands?" asked Mr. Klutz.

"Well, first of all," said Mrs. Lane, "he wants a panel of judges to decide the winner of the talent show, and he wants to be one of the judges."

"I have no problem with that," said Mr. Klutz. "What are his other two demands?"

"His second demand is that he wants every act in the talent show to mention

Porky's Pork Sausages at least once," said Mrs. Lane.

"Well . . . okay, I suppose we can do that," said Mr. Klutz. "After all, his company is sponsoring the show."

A bunch of other grown-ups came running in: Mr. Docker, Dr. Brad, Miss Lazar, Mr. Macky, Ms. Coco, Ms. Leaky, and Mrs. Cooney.

"We heard that *Ella Mentry School's Got Talent* is going to be on TV!" yelled Mr. Docker, our science teacher. "I can recite the periodic table of elements in order."*

"I can tap dance," said Ms. Coco, our gifted and talented teacher.

---

*Look it up!

"I can throw my voice," somebody said, but we didn't know who it was because they threw their voice.

"Yes, y'all can be in the talent show too," said Mrs. Lane.

"EEEEEK!" screamed our nurse, Mrs. Cooney. "I need to fix my hair."

"Why, is it broken?" I asked.

"Hold on a minute," said Mr. Klutz. "What is Mr. Porky's *third* demand?"

"Oh yes, there's one more thing that Mr. Porky wants before he'll put *Ella Mentry School's Got Talent* on TV," said Mrs. Lane. "He thinks it would be more exciting if the panel of judges could hit a big gong if they don't like an act. And if a contestant gets gonged, he or she gets thrown into a tank full of sharks."

WHAT?! That's got to be the dumbest idea in the history of the world!

"Is he nuts?" asked Mr. Klutz. "Mr. Porky wants to feed our students to sharks?"

"That's bananas!" said Ms. Hannah.

"That's loopy!" said Mrs. Roopy.

"Well, it doesn't *have* to be sharks," said Mrs. Lane. "It could be, oh, I don't know, vultures."

"He wants to feed our students to vultures?" asked Mr. Klutz.

"That's off the wall!" said Miss Small.

"That's loony!" said Mrs. Cooney.

"That's bizarre!" said Miss Lazar.

"Well, what if they were thrown into a pit of burning lava?" asked Mrs. Lane.

"That's wacky!" said Mr. Macky.

"That's loco!" said Ms. Coco.

"That's freaky!" said Ms. Leaky.

"Where would we possibly get a pit of burning lava anyway?" asked Mr. Klutz.

"We could go to Rent-A-Pit-Of-Burning-Lava," said Mrs. Lane. "You can rent anything."

"Are you off your rocker?" asked Mr. Docker.

"Have you gone mad?" asked Dr. Brad.

"That's *it*!" said Mr. Klutz angrily. "I'll give in to Mr. Porky's first two demands. But now I've got to draw the line. This is a school, not some silly TV show. You tell Mr. Porky that we say no. We're going to do *Ella Mentry School's Got Talent* without him. We don't care whether or not it's on TV! Who needs TV anyway?"

"Yeah, who needs TV?"

"Yeah, who needs TV?"

"Yeah, who needs TV?"

In case you were wondering, everybody was saying, "Yeah, who needs TV?"

Wait a minute. I need TV!

The World around Me

In the end, Mr. Porky backed down from his third demand. He agreed to put *Ella Mentry School's Got Talent* on TV even if the contestants were *not* attacked by sharks, vultures, or burning lava.

That was a relief, because I was sure to be the one who would get attacked by sharks, vultures, or burning lava. Nobody was laughing at my jokes at our last rehearsal. I was getting really nervous. *Ella Mentry School's Got Talent* was the next night, and I didn't have an act.

Mrs. Lane pulled me aside at the end of rehearsal.

"Y'know, nobody tells plain old jokes anymore, A.J.," she told me. "These days, comedians do what is called observational humor."

"What's *that*?" I asked.

"They sort of observe the world around them and talk about how funny it is," said Mrs. Lane. "Maybe you should try that, A.J."

I went home and observed the world around me. But my house wasn't very funny. My backyard wasn't very funny. My bedroom wasn't very funny. I didn't have anything funny to say.

I thought about it long and hard. I thought about it so hard that my brain hurt. Then I came to my decision—I was going to drop out of the talent show. Somebody else could win the secret grand prize.

The Big Night

Finally, the big night arrived. Even though I wasn't going to be in the talent show anymore, I came to school early and went backstage to help out with the lights, props, costumes, and stuff. There were TV cameras all over the place. Everybody was nervous.

I peeked at the audience from behind the curtain. The all-purpose room was packed. There must have been a million hundred people there. And a *billion* hundred would be watching on TV.

"We're gonna be famous!" Andrea said to anyone who would listen. "I'm so excited!"

Mr. Klutz climbed up on the stage. I saw the red lights on top of the TV cameras go on. That meant we were on TV! Some guy held up a sign that said APPLAUSE, and the audience started clapping and cheering.

"Welcome to *Ella Mentry School's Got Talent*," Mr. Klutz read from a cue card. "My name is Mr. Klutz, the school principal.

Before we get to our amazing talent,
I want to say one thing. Folks, do you
like pork sausages? I sure do. And when
I want a pork sausage, I reach for Porky's
Pork Sausages. They're the best pork

sausages in the world, made with the finest pork and no artificial ingredients. So when you want a pork sausage, reach for Porky's."

The guy held up the APPLAUSE sign again, and Mr. Klutz held up a package of Porky's Pork Sausages. Everybody clapped and cheered.

"Now it's time to announce the secret grand prize of *Ella Mentry School's Got Talent*," said Mr. Klutz.

Everybody got quiet, because they wanted to know what the secret grand prize would be.

"The winner of our talent show will receive a trophy and . . . a year's supply of

Porky's Pork Sausages!"

The guy held up the APPLAUSE sign, and everybody clapped and cheered, whether they liked pork sausages or not.

"Now it's time to introduce our panel

of judges," said Mr. Klutz. "Our first judge will be … Mr. Porky, the owner of Porky's Pork Sausages!"

A short, fat, bald guy came out and waved to the crowd.

He actually looked like a little pig.

"Our second judge will be ... Mrs. Lane!" said Mr. Klutz.

Mrs. Lane came out on roller skates while juggling flaming torches. She is *really* talented.

"It was Mrs. Lane who put this whole show together," said Mr. Klutz. "Would you like to say a few words?"

Mrs. Lane set her flaming torches down and roller-skated over to the microphone. But she didn't say a few words. She *sang* a few words to the tune of "Home on the Range." It went like this. . . .

"Oh give me some pork
with a knife and a fork,
and potatoes that have been French fried.
It makes a great lunch,
and I'll eat a whole bunch
with a plateful of beans on the side.
Porky's Pork Sausages.
I'd rather eat them than play.
And when I am done,
I'll take one on a bun
to bring home and to eat the next day."

Mrs. Lane is a really good singer. Everybody clapped and cheered for her.

"And now it's time to introduce our third judge," said Mr. Klutz, "who just happens to be our surprise celebrity guest."

"It's gonna be Mr. Hynde."

"It's gonna be Mr. Hynde."

"It's gonna be Mr. Hynde."

In case you were wondering, everybody was saying it was gonna be Mr. Hynde.

But everybody was wrong. So nah-nah-nah boo-boo on everybody.

"You all know him," said Mr. Klutz. "You all love him. Put your hands together for this year's hottest young rap sensation . . . Cray-Z!"

WHAT?!

Cray-Z is the coolest kid in the history of the world! A few months ago he came out with this rap song called "The Christmas

Klepto," and it was all over the radio, TV,
YouTube, magazines, *everywhere*. He's a
superstar!

"EEEEEEEK!" All the girls started
screaming, fainting, and freaking out.

"I love him!" some girl shouted.

"Marry me, Cray-Z!"

"That's right," said Mr. Klutz. "Cray-Z is in the house!"

Everybody went nuts when Cray-Z came out from the back of the all-purpose room. He was high-fiving kids and signing autographs.

The three judges sat at a table in front of the stage. Mr. Klutz explained the rules. . . .

"Each child blah blah blah blah two minutes blah blah blah blah at the end blah blah blah blah please do not take flash pictures blah blah blah blah our judges will decide blah blah blah blah blah . . ."

He went on for about a million hundred

hours. Nobody was paying attention.

"Okay, this is the moment you've all been waiting for," said Mr. Klutz. "It's time to bring on the talent! That is, right after this short message about Porky's Pork Sausages . . ."

Awesome-nificent

We had to sit through a boring commercial that explained why Porky's Pork Sausages were the best pork sausages in the world. Then Mrs. Lane introduced the acts, one at a time.

First, some boy came out and named all the presidents of the United States in order to the tune of "Yankee Doodle." Instead of James Polk, he said "James Pork."

Then some girl came out and wiggled her ears while she opened pistachio nuts inside her mouth without using her hands. That was weird.

After that five boys came out and banged on some garbage cans while shouting out the word "pork." I guess they couldn't think of anything else to do.

It was Alexia's turn. She came out with her skateboard, and we all gave her a big round of applause. Alexia is awesome on a skateboard. She did a bunch of cool tricks.

"I call this next trick the Sausage," she said.

Then she did a handstand on her skate-board. It was cool, and she got more applause.

"That's wonderful!" said Mrs. Lane.

Mrs. Lane introduced Andrea next, and Little Miss Know-It-All sang that awful "Tomorrow" song. But instead of singing about the sun coming out tomorrow, she

sang, "The pork will come out . . . tomorrow." It was embarrassing. Too bad Andrea wasn't thrown into a tank full of sharks.

There were a few more lame acts, and then Ryan came out and ate a chocolate-covered grasshopper. Ugh, gross! Emily did her dance from *The Little Mermaid*, and this time she didn't fall down. Neil the nude kid played the violin.

"Fantastic!" said Mrs. Lane after each act.

Next, a bunch of our teachers came out in giant hot dog bun costumes and put on a skit about sausages.

"That was amazing!" said Mrs. Lane. "Next up, we have a third grader in Mr. Granite's class who is going to do magic for us. Put your hands together for . . . Michael the Awesome-nificent!"

We all cheered, even though "awesome-nificent" is totally not a word. Michael made it up by putting "awesome" and "magnificent" together.*

---

*I told him it should be "magnif-awesome," but he wouldn't listen to me.

He came out wearing a black tuxedo. He looked like a penguin.

"Thank you," Michael said. "Watch me stand on my head!"

He drew a big picture of a face on a piece of paper, put it on the floor, and stepped on it. Everybody laughed.

"It's magic!" said Michael. "I will now make this ping-pong ball defy the laws of gravity."

He stood behind a desk and made the ping-pong ball float in the air above it. It was cool, even though it was obvious that Michael was holding a hair dryer under the desk.

"It's magic!" Michael said while everyone clapped. "You know, Porky's Pork Sausages come from pigs. So I will now make a pig disappear."

Michael held up a big red cloth and waved it around. Then he pulled it away like a bullfighter.

"It's magic!" Michael said. "Want to see me do it again?"

"Hey, you didn't make a pig disappear," some kid in the crowd yelled.

"Sure I did," Michael said. "It was an *invisible* pig."

He took a deep bow, and then Mrs. Lane roller-skated out on the stage again.

"Let's hear it for Michael the Awesomenificent!" she said. "Okay, our next talented performer is *another* third grader from Mr. Granite's class. Let's give him a warm welcome. Sit back and enjoy the comedy stylings of . . . A.J.!"

WHAT?!

Murder at the Talent Show

I thought I was gonna die.

"It's your turn, dude," Alexia said to me backstage. "Get out there."

"But I'm not *in* the talent show anymore!" I told her. "I dropped out."

The audience was clapping their hands. Mrs. Lane looked over at me.

"One more time," she announced. "Sit back and enjoy the comedy stylings of A.J.!"

I wanted to run away to Antarctica and go live with the penguins.

Mrs. Lane roller-skated over to me.

"What's the matter?" she asked.

"I don't have an act," I told her. "I dropped out."

"You never told me you were dropping out," she said.

"I forgot."

In the audience, people were stamping their feet and chanting, "A.J.! A.J.! A.J.!"

"They want you, A.J.!" said Mrs. Lane. "You can't let 'em down."

"You heard my jokes," I told her. "They were terrible. I'm afraid to go out there."

Mrs. Lane got down on one knee and put her arm around me.

"You know what?" she said. "When I was on *Are You Smarter Than a Turnip?*, I was afraid to go out there. When I was on *America's Not Stupid*, I was afraid to go out there. I was afraid to go out there when I was on *America's Next Top Garbage Collector, Keeping Up with the Librarians*, and *Who Wants to Win a Million Pizzas*, too. But you know what? I went out there anyway."

"And you won?" I asked.

"No, I lost on every one of those shows,"

she told me. "But *y'all* are going to be a star. Now go out there and kill 'em!"

"Kill 'em?" I asked. "I don't want to kill anybody."

"No, no," Mrs. Lane said. "When a comedian makes the audience laugh, they say he killed them. And when nobody laughs, they say he died out there."

Wow, I didn't know that comedy was so violent.

"A.J.! A.J.! A.J.!" people were chanting.

"This is no time to chicken out, A.J.," Mrs. Lane told me. "The show must go on. Now go out there and kill 'em!"

With that, she shoved me out on the stage.

Everybody clapped.

I looked around at all the people. They were all looking back at me.

I didn't know what to say. I didn't know what to do. I had to think fast.

"Uh . . . hi everybody," I said, tapping the microphone to make sure it worked.

"Hi!" the whole audience replied.

"I . . . uh . . . I'm not supposed to be here."

Everybody laughed even though I didn't say anything funny.

"This is weird," I said.

"What's weird?" somebody hollered.

"Everything," I said. "The school. The teachers. The all-purpose room. Hey, why do they call it the all-purpose room

anyway? It can't be used for *all* purposes. I mean, you can't go skydiving in here."

Some people actually laughed at that! I looked around the audience and saw Mr.

Klutz in the second row.

"You know what's *really* weird?" I asked. "Mr. Klutz, our principal. He's got no hair at all. I mean *none*! What's up with *that*?"

Mr. Klutz threw back his head and laughed. Somebody put a spotlight on him, and it reflected off his shiny head.

"Help! I'm going blind from the glare!" I said, covering my eyes. Everybody laughed. "Mr. Klutz must save a lot of money on shampoo and combs. They should use his head to bounce TV signals into outer space."

Everybody was cracking up. I looked backstage. The whole gang was behind the curtain giving me the thumbs-up sign.

"Mr. Klutz is nuts!" I continued. "Remember the time he got his foot caught in a rope, and he got stuck at the top of the flagpole? You should have *been* there! We were all glued to our seats. Well, not really. That would be weird. Why would anybody glue himself to a seat? How would you get the glue off?"

I had to stop for a few seconds because everybody was laughing so loud. Especially Mr. Klutz.

"But seriously," I said, "this other time, Mr. Klutz was climbing the side of the school when he got scared and couldn't go up or down. So our custodian, Miss Lazar, went up on the roof with a toilet bowl plunger. She stuck it on his bald head and lowered him to the ground. Miss Lazar should get the No Bell Prize, if you ask me. That's a prize they give out to people who don't have bells."

The audience was eating it up!

"You rock, A.J.!" somebody shouted.

I told a few more stories about the weird things grown-ups have done at our school. Like the time our groundskeeper, Mr. Burke, discovered gold buried in the playground. And the time our security guard, Officer Spence, threw all the teach- ers in jail for stealing peanut butter and jelly sandwiches.

When I couldn't think of other weird

stories to tell, I looked over at Mrs. Lane.

"Keep going!" she said.

I noticed Mr. Porky at the judges' table. He had an angry look on his face. That's when I remembered that every act had to mention pork sausages.

"There's just one more thing I want to say," I said. "I love Porky's Pork Sausages!"

I ran off the stage, and everybody hugged me. It was the greatest night of my life.

"A.J., you killed 'em!" Mrs. Lane said.

The Big Surprise Ending

There were a few more acts after that, but I wasn't paying any attention to them. Everybody was coming over to slap me on the back and tell me how much they liked my comedy routine.

"You are totally going to win this thing, dude," said Alexia. "You were awesome."

Before that could happen, we had to have the big grand finale. Everybody who was part of the show—kids, teachers, judges, the stage crew—came out onstage. We all sang the Porky's Pork Sausages theme song. It was loud! Some of the teachers were dancing. The crowd was clapping and stamping their feet. Cray-Z was playing bongos on Mr. Klutz's head. It was cool.

And it was over. Mr. Klutz made the shut-up peace sign and asked Mr. Porky to come over to the microphone. He had a trophy in one hand and an envelope in his other hand.

"Thank you!" Mr. Porky said. "This has

been a wonderful evening. It's clear that you have a lot of talent here at Ella Mentry School, and you all love Porky's Pork Sausages. But now it's time to announce the winner of *Ella Mentry School's Got Talent*."

I hope I win. I hope I win. I hope I win. I hope I win. I hope I win.

"The winner is . . ."

Everybody got quiet as Mr. Porky tore open the envelope. You could have heard a pin drop in the all-purpose room.

Well, that is if anybody had pins with them. But why would anybody bring pins to a talent show? That would be weird.

Anyway, there was electricity in the air. Well, not really, because if there was electricity in the air, we all would have been electrocuted.

What I mean to say is, everybody in the audience was on pins and needles.

Well, not really. They were sitting on seats. It would have hurt if they were on pins and needles.

I bet you're dying to know who won the talent show, aren't you?

Well, I'm not going to tell you.

Okay, okay, I'll tell you.

"The winner is . . . ," said Mr. Porky, "Mrs. Penny Lane!"

WHAT!?

"But she's one of the judges!" Ryan shouted.

"That's not fair!" shouted Michael.

Everybody started yelling, screaming, and freaking out. Mrs. Lane had a big smile on her face as she roller-skated over to get her prize.

"The talent show was supposed to be for kids!" complained Andrea. "Grown-ups can't win!"

"Says who?" said Mrs. Lane as she grabbed the trophy. "Gimme that!"

"BOOOOOOOOOO!"

"My daughter should have been the winner!" shouted one of the parents in the audience. "Mrs. Lane is a fraud!"

"She must have made a secret deal with Mr. Porky!" somebody else shouted.

"That's the only reason she won!"

What a scam. Mrs. Lane took the microphone.

"I'd like to thank all the little people who made this possible," she said. "I was the loser on *Are You Smarter Than a Turnip?* I was the loser on *America's Not Stupid.* And I was the loser on *Keeping Up with the Librarians* and *America's Next Top Garbage Collector* and *Who Wants to Win a Million Pizzas?* and *Undercover Mother.* But tonight I'm the winner, whether you like it or not!"

"The talent show was fixed!" shouted one of the parents. "Stop her!"

"Run for it, Penny!" shouted Mr. Porky.

A bunch of angry parents got up from their seats and came charging toward the stage. Mrs. Lane roller-skated toward the exit door, grabbing a box of pork sausages on her way out.

And that was the last we ever saw of her.

Maybe the parents will catch up with Mrs. Lane and take the trophy away from her. Maybe we'll have another talent show next year. Maybe Mr. Klutz will stop hiding in the bushes. Maybe Mrs. Lane will stop saying "y'all" and turning her eyelids inside out. Maybe Mrs. Cooney will fix her broken hair. Maybe people will stop discriminating against different kinds of farts. Maybe Mr. Porky will get attacked by sharks, vultures, or burning lava. Maybe Andrea will finally stop singing songs from *Annie*. Maybe we'll get some free pork sausages. Maybe people will stop eating bugs to get on TV. Maybe Michael

will make a pig disappear. Maybe mon-
keys will stop dropping dead and falling
out of trees. Maybe they'll use Mr. Klutz's
head to bounce TV signals into outer
space. Maybe people will stop running
into doors. Maybe we'll get to skydive in
the all-purpose room.

But it won't be easy!